B
11-10-03

# HEART OF A TIGER

*Marsha Diane Arnold*
*pictures by* Jamichael Henterly

DIAL BOOKS FOR YOUNG READERS

NEW  YORK

*To Amy and Cal, for their inspiration*
*To Diane Arico, for her faith* —M.D.A.

*To my siblings seven* —J.H.

―――――――――

*Special thanks to Dr. Laxmi G. Tewari, Professor of India Studies at Sonoma State University,*
*for generously translating the animal names into Hindi and informing me of the ritual* Namakarana.

―――――――――

Published by Dial Books for Young Readers
A member of Penguin Putnam Inc.
375 Hudson Street • New York, New York 10014

Text copyright © 1995 by Marsha Arnold
Pictures copyright © 1995 by Jamichael Henterly
All rights reserved • Design by Nancy R. Leo
Manufactured in China
First Edition
7 9 10 8 6

Library of Congress Cataloging in Publication Data
Arnold, Marsha Diane.
Heart of a tiger / by Marsha Diane Arnold ; pictures by Jamichael Henterly.
— 1st ed. p.  cm.
Summary: As the Name Day celebration approaches, a young kitten tries to deserve
a noble name, by following the path of the beautiful Bengal tiger.
ISBN 0-8037-1695-8.— ISBN 0-8037-1696-6 (lib. ed.)
[1. Cats—Fiction. 2. Tigers—Fiction. 3. Names, Personal—Fiction. 4. India—Fiction]
I. Henterly, Jamichael, ill. II. Title.
PZ7.A7363He 1995  [E]—dc20  94-17126  CIP  AC

*The paintings for this book were done in watercolor on Arches hot-pressed watercolor paper.*

## Pronunciation Guide

| Visvasi Naukar | vish-VA-see NOW-cur |
| Bahadur Shikari | ba-ha-DUR shi-car-EE |
| Rang Birange Kapare | raNNg bee-raNNg-gay ka-pa-RAY |
| Sailani | SAW-la-nee |
| Bangali Sher Ka Dil | ban-GA-lee SHEEr KA dill |

Among the animals there is a custom.
Names are not given on the day of their birth,
for even a mother cannot tell what is a fitting
name for one so recently arrived. When
a year has passed, a Name Day Celebration
is held and each animal born the previous spring
chooses its own name. But the young one
may only keep that name if all the animals
agree it is a fair and honest name.

V ISVASI AND HER KITTENS SCATTERED as Master pushed the door open and stomped past them. He had risen early to hunt jungle fowl for his family's dinner table.

Number Four hid himself under a pillow, for he had heard the loud boom of Master's gun before and he did not like it.

As the rumbling of Master's jeep faded into the forest, the kittens returned to more important matters. The Name Day Celebration was only one week away.

"My name shall be Bahadur Shikari—Mighty Hunter," declared Number One, scouting the veranda for mice.

"I'll choose Rang Birange Kapare—Calico Colors," added Number Two as she sat grooming her long fur.

"Sailani—Adventurer—will be my name," called Number Three from high in the jasmine trellis.

"And you, Number Four," asked Two, turning to the small gray kitten who had finally pulled his head from beneath the pillow. "What will your name be? Smallest of All?"

"Why…well…my…I haven't decided," he mumbled as he straightened himself and stared into the forest.

Being the runt of the litter, Four supposed he should name himself Smallest of All. But he was afraid if he named himself that, it would always be so.

"What are you looking at, out there in the forest, day after day?" asked Two.

"The sunlight and the shadows and the cotton tree flowers," Four answered.

His answer was the truth. But it was not all the truth. When Four stared into the forest, he was doing more than looking. He was searching.

He had seen the Magnificent One pass this way, golden stripes shining like a hundred suns amid black night, steps floating smooth and silent through tender grass.

Four felt from the first time he had seen the Wondrous Beast that this is what he was meant to be. Not Smallest of All or Tiny Gray Thing, but Golden Splendor…Silent Walker…Beautiful Bengal.

Yet Four had never found the courage to follow and to learn, and now Naming Day was only one week away.

As the sun's first rays lit the sky, the lights and shades of the forest began to play tricks. Four did not stop to think of the dangers of the forest or the comfort of his pillow. One week before Naming Day was all he thought, and he ran deep into the forest in search of Beautiful Bengal.

When he reached the shade of a bombax tree, Four looked up and saw a flock of parakeets preening themselves.

"What are you doing so far from the plantation?" said one.

"I'm searching for Bengal," Four answered, "so I can learn to be like him and give myself a name like his on Naming Day."

The parakeets twittered uncontrollably, nearly falling from their perches.

"Do you see my bright feathers?" chirped one. "Without them I would not be a parakeet. And in your murky gray coat you will never be a tiger."

With this, all the parakeets shrieked, "Murky Gray Coat, Murky Gray Coat."

Four peered at his reflection in a rain puddle. He sat for awhile, stared again into the forest, then rose and walked determinedly on.

In and around a zizyphus tree, long-tailed langurs lunched.

"What is this small gray spot among the fallen fruit?" asked one of the langurs.

"It's me, Four. I'm searching for Bengal so I can learn to be like him and give myself a name like his on Naming Day."

The langur chuckled and chattered. "The Bengal tiger would eat me in two bites. But you, Little Gray Spot, he would eat you in *one*."

All the monkeys broke into rude laughter.

"One Morsel should be your name....One Morsel, One Morsel," they teased.

"And your names should be The Messy Ones," said Four, but the langurs did not hear. Their laughter turned to screeching as they scrambled to the highest branches. "Ka-kao-ka, ka-kao-ka."

Quickly Four turned. Two yellow-green eyes glowed stern before him. A golden forehead wrinkled in annoyance. White teeth flashed.

"Your meddling has cost me my dinner!" Bengal's voice was like thunder. "Who are you and why do you scurry through my forest?"

Four squeezed a tiny sound from his quivering throat. "I am Four. I came to the forest to learn from you, so I can give myself a tiger's name on Naming Day."

Bengal cocked his head. "You are no tiger."

Four found more courage. "You can teach me to be."

"How can one teach wisdom? How can one teach bravery?"

"I will follow you and watch."

"I travel far and I travel alone."

"I will not ruin your dinner again," Four promised. "Oh, Bengal, I cannot live with a small, gray, ordinary name. In my heart I am bigger than what you see."

Bengal's eyes softened, but his voice was firm. "Return to your mother, Little Four, before it is too late." Silently he glided into the yellow-brown thicket and disappeared.

In the distance came a peacock's cry, "Naming Day, Naming Day."

"One week away," answered Four, and he sprang through the thicket after Beautiful Bengal.

Days and nights, Four followed Bengal. His paws became bruised, his fur grew matted, and his stomach was sometimes empty.

But he learned much. Much about when to be silent in the forest, where the best water holes were, and how to live wisely and strongly on his own.

After a time Four became too weary to keep up. Walking across the flat grassland, he came upon a large rock and crawled into its high crevice to rest.

"Tomorrow I will track Bengal and find him again," he said as he curled his tail around his nose and fell asleep.

Barrrr-rrrrum, Barrrr-rrrrum. Clang-BANG-Clang.
Barrrr-rrrrum, Barrrr-rrrrum. Clang-BANG-Clang.
Four woke to see men moving steadily across the savannah.
Tin cans rattled at their sides. Sticks and spoons and pipes beat
against drums and pots and pans. The savannah filled with a deafening
clamor.

Where the river ran, at the other side of the savannah, Four saw elephants lumbering toward the beaters, elephants unlike those he had often seen passing through the forest. These elephants carried large, decorated baskets on their backs and their jewel-covered skins sparkled in the light. Squinting his eyes against the sun, Four saw that the baskets held men and the men held…guns!

Four shrank into his crevice. A streak of orange and black veered toward him. It was Bengal, zigzagging from thicket to thicket, trying to escape the endless noise by running toward the river.

At that moment Four understood the terrible trick the men were playing.

As Bengal neared the rock, Four gave one strong leap and landed on the tiger's back. Clinging tightly, he moved close to Bengal's ear. "Bengal, it is Four. Listen to me and you will live."

Bengal ran on. "I must reach the river and swim to safety before the Terrible Noise swallows us."

"No, Bengal. The elephants block the river."

"I have walked before among elephants," the tiger insisted.

Four spoke more firmly. "Upon these elephants ride men, and in their hands is death. I saw them from my perch high on the rock."

Bengal slowed his pace and listened.

"The beaters are loud and frightening," said Four, "but they are only noise. Trust me, Bengal. Turn and run toward the beaters."

Bengal thought for only a moment. Then he turned toward the beaters and ran.

Screaming in terror, the beaters darted in all directions. Sticks and spoons and pipes flew into thickets. Drums and pots and pans dropped in the grass.

The men with guns were left alone on the far side of the savannah.

Together Four and Bengal found a safe place in the forest and collapsed near a clump of bamboo.

"Did you see their faces, Bengal?" asked Four with a twinkle in his eye. "We played a trick on them the way they tried to play a trick on you."

"It would have been a deadly trick if you had not been there," panted Bengal.

When dusk approached, Bengal rose and said, "Little Four, you wanted a name like mine on Naming Day. But I fear you will never be a Bengal tiger. You will never be ten feet long. You will never have a coat of a hundred suns amid black night."

Four looked down at his small body and gray coat. Even with all he had learned, with all he had done, he knew Bengal spoke the truth.

"But inside, Little Four, you have a heart that will grow in wisdom and power as you grow."

Bengal turned toward the plantation. "Your Naming Day is almost here. You would not want to miss it."

On Naming Day the Indian sun woke the plantation early. From forest and farm the animals gathered near the banyan tree for the celebration. One by one Visvasi Naukar—Faithful Servant—proudly introduced her kittens by their chosen names:

Bahadur Shikari—Mighty Hunter
Rang Birange Kapare—Calico Colors
Sailani—Adventurer
and
Bangali Sher Ka Dil—Heart of a Tiger.

And all the animals agreed they were fair and honest names.

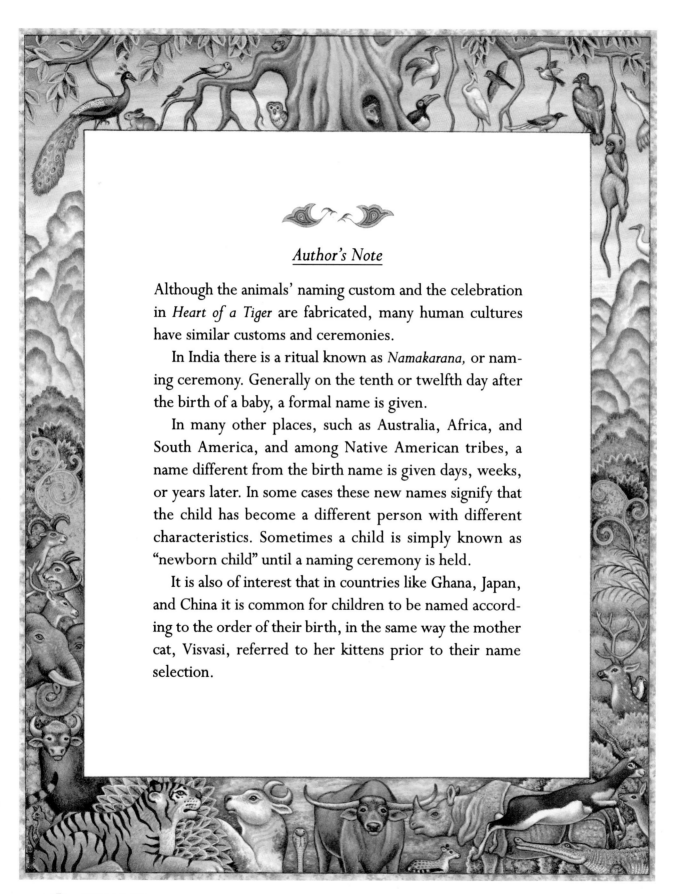

## Author's Note

Although the animals' naming custom and the celebration in *Heart of a Tiger* are fabricated, many human cultures have similar customs and ceremonies.

In India there is a ritual known as *Namakarana,* or naming ceremony. Generally on the tenth or twelfth day after the birth of a baby, a formal name is given.

In many other places, such as Australia, Africa, and South America, and among Native American tribes, a name different from the birth name is given days, weeks, or years later. In some cases these new names signify that the child has become a different person with different characteristics. Sometimes a child is simply known as "newborn child" until a naming ceremony is held.

It is also of interest that in countries like Ghana, Japan, and China it is common for children to be named according to the order of their birth, in the same way the mother cat, Visvasi, referred to her kittens prior to their name selection.